9·2010

Happy Birthday!
Enjoy reading! ♥, Eiša

For Elinor, Charlie, and Lee,
who are always good eggs, often silly geese, and sometimes
(in the best possible way) odd ducks

Published in the United States of America by Schwartz &
Wade Books, an imprint of Random House Children's
Books, a division of Random House, Inc., New York.
SCHWARTZ & WADE BOOKS and colophon are trademarks
of Random House, Inc.

www.randomhouse.com/kids
Educators and librarians, for a variety of teaching tools,
visit us at www.randomhouse.com/teachers

The text of this book is set in Bodoni Old Face.
The illustrations are rendered in oil paint.

Library of Congress Cataloging-in-Publication Data
Hills, Tad.
Duck & Goose / Tad Hills.— 1st ed.
p. cm.

Summary: Duck and Goose learn to work
together to take care of a ball,
which they think is an egg.

ISBN 0-375-83611-X (alk. paper)
ISBN 0-375-93611-4 (lib. bdg.)

[1. Interpersonal relations—Fiction. 2. Ducks—Fiction.
3. Geese—Fiction.] I. Title: Duck and Goose. II. Title.
PZ7.H563737 Duc 2006
[E]—dc22
2005010849

MANUFACTURED IN CHINA
5 6 7 8 9 10
First Edition

Duck & Goose

written & illustrated by Tad Hills

schwartz & wade books · new york

"Oh my, what is that?" Duck quacked.

"THAT's a silly question," Goose honked. "It is a big egg, of course."

"Of course it is an egg. I know that!" huffed Duck. "What I mean is, where did it come from?"

Goose looked skyward. He looked to the river. He looked to the fields. He thought very hard. "Who are you?" he asked finally.

"I," said Duck, puffing out his feathered chest, "am the one whose egg this is.

I saw it first."

Goose quickly raised one webbed foot. "It's mine.

I touched it first."

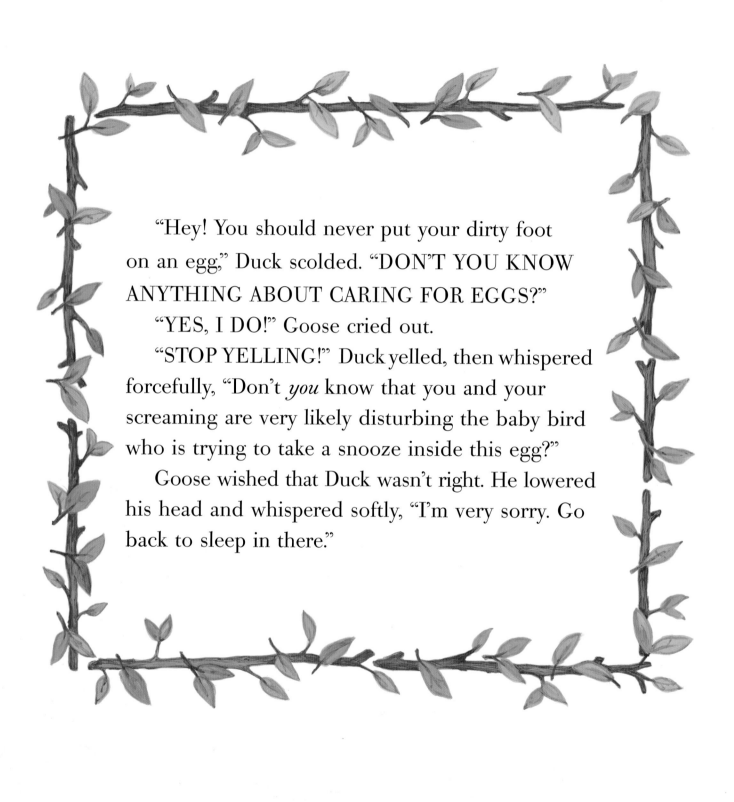

"Hey! You should never put your dirty foot on an egg," Duck scolded. "DON'T YOU KNOW ANYTHING ABOUT CARING FOR EGGS?"

"YES, I DO!" Goose cried out.

"STOP YELLING!" Duck yelled, then whispered forcefully, "Don't *you* know that you and your screaming are very likely disturbing the baby bird who is trying to take a snooze inside this egg?"

Goose wished that Duck wasn't right. He lowered his head and whispered softly, "I'm very sorry. Go back to sleep in there."

"My, that's quite a beauty you have," called a blue bird from across the river.

"Thank you, it's mine," quacked Duck.

"Actually, it's mine," honked Goose. "Thank you."

"So," asked Duck, "what do we do now?"

"We should do something," suggested Goose.

"Yes, you are right, good thinking," agreed Duck.

"Like what?"

Duck and Goose each thought.

"Well, we must keep the egg warm until the fuzzy little occupant is ready to come out," said Goose.

"Excellent idea!" exclaimed Duck.

He pushed past Goose.

"Step aside and I shall do just that."

But Goose was quick, too.

After a flurry of fussing,

grunting and groaning,

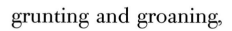

slipping and sliding,

honking and quacking,

Duck and Goose found themselves back to back.

"Scoot over, I don't have any room!" complained Duck.

"You are much closer to me than I am to you."

"Stop yelling in my ear, Goose!"

"Shhhhh . . . ," Goose hushed, pointing at the round thing beneath them.

"Yes, yes, yes, we must remember. Quiet, quiet, quiet, we mustn't disturb the little one."

And so they sat, very still and very quiet, waiting.

For a long time they waited.

They listened to the crickets chirp and the frogs burp.

"I am going to teach this baby bird to quack like a duck," Duck boasted.

"Well, I am going to teach it to honk like a goose," Goose honked back.

"I'm going to teach this baby bird to waddle," Goose added.

"So am I," Duck said.

They heard the pitter-patter of the rain.

"I'm going to teach this baby bird to swim," Duck said.

"Me too," Goose said.

To pass the time, they sniffed wildflowers in the warm sun and shared breadcrumbs while Goose taught Duck to honk.

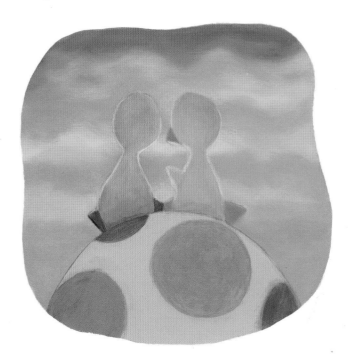

They watched the sun set in the sky, and Duck taught Goose to quack.

They counted the stars in
the night sky.

"Let's teach our baby to fly,"
said Goose.

"Good idea," said Duck.

"I'm sure our baby will be a
fast learner," said Duck.

"If it takes after you and me,
I'm sure you're right,"
agreed Goose.

Together they waited, until—
"Did you feel that, Duck?"
Duck nodded. "Yes! Did you feel that, Goose?"
Goose nodded.
"It's time, Goose, it's time!" Duck squawked.

Quickly, Duck slid down and started
running in circles around their egg.

"What should we do now?"

he hollered.

"I think we should remain calm,"

Goose yelled back.

"Excuse me," a little voice called out.

Duck stopped. In all the exciting confusion, he had failed to notice the blue bird kicking their egg.

"Can I play, too?" she asked.

"**Play?** This is no time for play!" yelled Duck.

"THIS IS NO TIME FOR GAMES!" yelled Goose. "And what's with the kicking?"

"I was only trying to get your attention," said the little bird.

"Well, you got it!" Duck huffed. "False alarm, Goose. Back to work."

"Can't you see that we are very busy here?" Goose explained to the blue bird. "This is serious business. This is perhaps the most important moment of our lives."

"Oh my, I am sorry," apologized the blue bird. "I had no idea. I just thought that maybe I could play with your ball. "It really is a nice one," she added, and then she flew away.

Goose gulped.

"Did she say 'ball'?" he whispered to Duck.

"You know, I did have my doubts," Duck finally said. "It is a bit squishier than most eggs I've seen."

"Yes, and I must say, I was somewhat suspicious of those big dots," Goose admitted.

"It may not be an egg, but it is lovely," said Duck.

"Oh, absolutely, Duck," Goose agreed. "It's a keeper."

As the crickets chirped, the frogs burped, and the grass swayed in a gentle breeze, Goose quacked and Duck honked, and the ball bounced, rolled, and sometimes . . .

even flew.